INSATIABLE

and Other Stories

Blessings,
Jack Clubb

by Jack Clubb

NEWMAN SPRINGS PUBLISHING
320 Broad Street
Red Bank, NJ 07701

First originally published by Newman Springs Publishing 2021

(The following stories are presented as fiction
although some are inspired by actual events.)

ISBN 978-1-63881-212-8 (Paperback)
ISBN 978-1-63881-213-5 (Digital)

Printed in the United States of America

This book is dedicated to the Hollywood Writers
Group and its shepherd, John Frank

ABOUT THE AUTHOR

Jack Clubb has been published in the United States, the United Kingdom, and India. You may find his stories in back issues of *Black Creek Review, Coffee-Ground Breakfast, The Magic of Words, Northern Stars, Opinion Magazine, Pancakes in Heaven, Rockford Review, The Storyteller, Sunrise, The Taylor Trust,* and *Voices from the Valley.*

Jack's poetry can be found in such places as *Art With Words, Bell's Letters, Black Creek Review, The Cabell Standard* (West Virginia Newspaper), *Candelabrum* (Britain), *California Quarterly of the California State Poetry Society, Coffee-Ground Breakfast, Harp Strings, The Hatchling, Lucidity, The Lyric, The Magic of Words, Metverse Muse* (India), *Midwest Poetry Review, Moments, New Writers Magazine, Northern Stars, The Oak, Opinion Magazine, Parnassus Literary Journal, Pegasus, Penny Dreadful, Piedmont Literary Review, Poetry Digest, Poets' Digest, Poet's Paper, Poetry in Motion, The Putnam Standard* (West Virginia newspaper), *Riverrun, Rubies in the Darkness* (Britain), *Snippets, Songs of Innocence, SP Quill Magazine, Star Poets, Theme Poetry, Tradition,* and *Westward Quarterly.*

Jack has received awards from Black Creek Review, The Lyric, Moments, Northern Stars, and Perry County Writers Guild.

jackclubb@peoplepc.com

CONTENTS

INSATIABLE

Harriette and Herman Glickson were seated in their living room on matching easy chairs which Harriette had reupholstered in blue velvet. A small table was between the chairs, which held their glasses of iced tea. It was an extremely hot day.

Harriette looked up from a magazine she was reading. "You know, Herman, I am so proud of Lester. He's not laid-back like you. His quest for money is insatiable."

"I'm not laid-back. What do you mean by that remark?"

"Yes, you are laid-back. You're content just to have a comfortable little job in an office and collect a paycheck."

"It's a good paycheck."

"Good enough, I suppose. But look at Lester. He lives in a twenty-five thousand square foot mansion that's beautifully furnished. We live in this small, cramped house, which is only nicely furnished because I reupholster furniture I buy at second-hand stores."

"The only furniture you reupholstered is our living-room suite."

"That's because our house is so small we don't have much room for furniture."

"Gripe and complain, Harriette. Gripe and complain."

"What else can I do when I see what our son has? But, of course, Lester doesn't get his drive from you. He gets it from my side of the family. My father always had plenty of money."

"Your father was jailed for embezzlement."

"My father was framed for embezzlement."

"Have it your own way, Harriette. Have it your own way."

The doorbell rang.

"That must be our handsome, incredibly wealthy son," Harriette said.

"I guess he wants to visit his ugly, impoverished father," Herman replied.

"Oh, stop it!" Harriette admonished. "You may be poor, but you're not ugly."

Herman smiled. "At least I win on one count."

Lester seated himself on the blue velvet couch. Harriette brought him a glass of iced tea from the kitchen and set it on the coffee table.

"I don't know how you two can stand this heat," Lester said. "I dread coming here in summer."

"I keep begging your father to install air conditioning, but it's no go. Instead, we just sit here and drink iced tea."

"Well, anytime you want, you can come to my house to cool off."

"That's so thoughtful of you, Lester," Harriette said. "I'm always raving to everyone about your forty-room house."

"It's nice to have plenty of space," Lester said. "I don't know how you two survive in these cramped quarters."

Herman spoke: "Lester, you grew up here in these cramped quarters."

"I know, but I always hated being poor."

"We weren't poor."

"Well, we didn't live under a freeway bridge, but this neighborhood is best described as ordinary."

"What's wrong with being ordinary?"

"Nothing at all if you have no ambition."

"How are things going with your business?" Harriette asked.

"The investment company's doing just fine, and I'm in the process of buying another apartment building."

"I'm so proud of you," Harriette said. "Nicole is lucky to have you."

"Nicole and I are thinking about getting a divorce."

"Good," Harriette said. "I never liked her anyway. You deserve better."

Six months later, Harriette met Herman at their front door when he was coming home from work.

"Sit down, Herman. I have the most appalling news. Nicole's been arrested."

"Arrested!"

"Yes, arrested. Her attorney telephoned me because he wants us to put up bail. According to the attorney, Lester and Nicole were running a Ponzi scheme."

"What's a Ponzi scheme?"

"I'm surprised you don't know. According to the attorney, when people deposited funds in Lester's investment company, some of the funds were siphoned off for Lester and Nicole's personal use. Other funds were used to pay investors dividends; but no funds were actually invested, so the investment company never made a profit. Eventually, the company would collapse if too many investors withdrew their funds at once."

"Where is Lester?" Herman asked.

"No one knows. The attorney thinks he's gone to Argentina because he has friends there."

"I'm glad his nanny spoke to him in Spanish when he was young. He speaks it pretty well."

"The awful thing," Harriette continued, "is that beautiful mansion and all Lester's apartment buildings will go back to the bank. Without the funds from the investment company, there is no way to pay the mortgages."

"It sounds like our adorable son is a crook," Herman said.

"Of course Lester's not a crook," Harriette replied. "This is all Nicole's doing. I hope she rots in jail. No wonder Lester wants to divorce her."

"I wonder how Lester will do in Argentina."

"He'll do very well," Harriette said. "When your drive for money is insatiable, you always succeed. It's in your nature."

"I may be laid-back," Herman replied, "but at least I'm not being pursued by the police."

"And we'll never live in a mansion either. I don't know why I ever chained myself to a man who has no ambition."

"Well, you did, Harriette, so don't complain."

THE PIANO

Allen heard his son, Jason, playing the piano in the den. Jason's mother, Cassandra, was seated on an easy chair near the piano. Her eyes were closed. She looked like she was in ecstasy.

Allen went into the den. "Jason, would you stop that racket! It's driving me crazy!"

Jason stopped playing. Cassandra spoke: "Stop that racket? What do you mean, Al? That's the 'Moonlight Sonata.' Wait till Jason gets to the difficult third movement. He does it brilliantly."

"First, second, third movement! I don't care what he does as long as he stops that infernal noise."

"Noise? It's not noise," Cassandra replied. "It's one of Beethoven's most beautiful sonatas."

"Beethoven, shmatoven! I don't care what it is. I just want it stopped."

"The trouble with you, Al, is that you have no appreciation for culture. You just want to sit in front of the TV and watch sports. We never go to the opera or ballet."

"Opera! Ballet! Who on earth cares about those things?"

"Sensible, educated people love opera and ballet. I'm going to start taking Jason to the Music Center now that he's older."

"I thought Jason was studying to be an electrician."

Jason spoke: "I am, Father, but I find it boring."

"Boring? How could electricity be boring?"

"I'm sure Jason will be a brilliant electrician," Cassandra said, "but right now I would like to hear him play the 'Moonlight Sonata.'"

"At least Jason can make a good salary as an electrician," Allen said. "No one makes much money from music."

"I made money when I played the piano at The Green Room," Cassandra replied.

"I thought you just worked for tips."

"I did, but they were generous tips. People love music in spite of what you say."

"Now that Jason's studying electricity," Allen said, "perhaps he can put a twenty-amp line in the kitchen for the microwave. This old house has only sixty amps. It's time we updated."

"Don't you think Jason should wait until he gets his contractor's license?"

"That will take forever."

Two weeks later, Jason and his mother went to see a production of *Lucia* at the Music Center. Cassandra looked radiant in a long white evening dress, and Jason looked dashing in his navy blue suit.

"Lucia was so sensible," Cassandra said when the opera was over. "I should have killed my husband on our wedding night like she did. He is such a drag."

"Then I wouldn't have been born," Jason replied.

Cassandra smiled. "That's true. At least I got something good out of the deal."

"I've always tried to make Dad happy, but he's so hard to please. I put the twenty-amp line in the kitchen while you were at work today, but I doubt if he'll give me any praise for my effort."

"He's never happy," Cassandra replied. "That man was born to complain. I think his mother was glad I took him off her hands."

When Jason and his mother arrived home, they found fire trucks in front of their house. Allen was in the front yard.

"Look what you've done, you stupid idiot!" Allen screamed as Jason and his mother walked from their parked car to the front gate. "The house would have burned down if I hadn't been here to call the fire department."

"I told you not to let Jason do electrical work until he had his contractor's license," Cassandra said, "but you wouldn't listen. You're as stubborn as a mule."

"Oh, so blame this on me! Jason's an idiot, and you're his idiot mother!"

"Don't you dare speak to me that way!" Cassandra replied.

"I'll speak to you any way I want to. I'm just glad Jason's not my son. I could never have fathered such a fool."

Jason looked at his mother. "Does he mean I'm really not his son?"

Cassandra flushed red. She hesitated before she spoke. "The fertility clinic said Al couldn't be a father, so he's your legal father but not your biological father, and I can't say I'm unhappy about it. I couldn't deal with a son as cranky as Al is."

"Then Lucia could have killed her husband on her wedding night and still given birth to a son if they had fertility clinics in seventeenth-century Scotland."

"She could, but I don't want to think about it. Let's just say that I don't think you should become an electrician. It's not your strong point."

"Somehow, Mother, I completely agree."

THE TREE

"I don't see how we can afford to keep this house."

"Don't tell me that, Dirk. That's not what I want to hear."

"Once the title is transferred to your name, Brenda, the house will be reappraised, and the taxes will be massive."

"This is where I grew up, Dirk. The house means so much to me. But even more than the house, I love the tree in the backyard. I used to sit under the tree when I was small, and Mother would read me stories. All of our cats are buried there. Mother sat under the tree when she became ill. She loved the tree as much as I do."

"That tree is over forty feet tall. It should be trimmed."

"I would never let anyone touch that tree. I love it too much."

Dirk and Brenda were sitting in the cavernous living room of her mother's house.

"What a dilemma," Brenda said. "We inherit a house, and we can't afford to keep it."

"There's not only the taxes and insurance," Dirk said. "There are the mortgage payments that have to be paid each month. Where on earth will we get the money?"

"Mother warned me not to marry you, Dirk. I can see now that she was right. I should have married someone with better prospects."

"What your mother did was unfair. She left the house to you and gave the money to your brother."

"She felt sorry for Bart," Brenda said. "He couldn't hold a job. He was even poorer than you in spite of having a good education."

Dirk loved the magnificent mansion. There were thirty large rooms, every one of them beautifully furnished. The afternoon sun was streaming through the huge living-room window, bathing him and Brenda in glorious sunlight as they sat on the red velvet wing chairs.

"Our apartment is so small," Brenda said. "I just can't believe we can't find a way to live here."

"It's really depressing," Dirk said. "Totally depressing."

A week later, when Dirk came home from work, Brenda met him at the door of their apartment.

"I have the most wonderful news," Brenda said. "We can keep Mother's house after all."

"We can?"

"Yes, I spoke to my brother, and he says if I add his name to the deed, he will pay the mortgage and taxes on Mother's house."

"Will he want to live with us?"

"Of course."

"I don't think this is a good idea, Brenda. Your brother's drunk most of the time, and he's a troublemaker. He'll quarrel with all our neighbors."

"That's nonsense. Bart may take a drink once in a while, but that's okay. He can stay in an upstairs bedroom. I'll put a complete liquor cabinet in his room so he doesn't have to wander all over the house looking for something to drink."

"Will your brother promise to take a bath?"

"Oh, stop it, Dirk! This is our one chance to have a truly beautiful home. Don't blow it by creating roadblocks."

Before Bart moved in, Benda showed Dirk the liquor cabinet she had purchased for the upstairs bedroom. It was six feet high and stocked with every kind of liquor and wine.

"Isn't it gorgeous, Dirk? I've spent a fortune on alcohol, thanks to my credit cards. There's bourbon, scotch, gin, vodka, rum, and forty different kinds of wine, and they're all good brands too. Bart should be very happy."

"He'll be so happy he'll never leave his room," Dirk said.

Brenda smiled evilly. "That's the general idea."

Dirk and Brenda were extremely happy in their new home. Dirk loved the antiques, the beautiful porcelain figures, and the replica of the clock Marie Antoinette had at Versailles. But best of all, Bart stayed in his own room. He had no reason to leave it since he no longer had any need to work, and he had the fried chicken he was so fond of delivered to the door. His girlfriend, Suzanne, came by at regular intervals and stayed the night. She was unfriendly and rarely spoke.

Two years later, there was a storm, a storm to end all storms. There was a crash. The house shook violently. Brenda and Dirk ran into the backyard.

"The tree, Dirk! The tree! It's fallen onto the house!"

Brenda and Dirk ran up to Bart's room. The tree had crashed through the ceiling and knocked the liquor cabinet over. They pushed the cabinet up. Bart was underneath covered in blood, liquor, and broken bottles.

"How awful, Dirk. I never expected Bart to go this way! I thought he'd live a long life, drinking contentedly."

"In a way, Brenda, he drank himself to death. The tree and the liquor cabinet were the final touch."

"The way the rain is pouring into this room, the house will be ruined. I was supposed to pay the homeowner's insurance, but I forgot. Bart said that was to be my contribution for the upkeep of the house."

"With damage this massive, perhaps we should sell and buy another mansion."

"We can't really."

"Why not?"

"Bart insisted I title the deed so that his half would remain in his estate if he died."

"You mean, you only own half the house even though Bart is dead?"

"That's correct."

"Who gets the other half?"

"Suzanne. She's Bart's executrix and sole heir. She gets all the money, everything."

"Why on earth would he do that?"

"It was the only way Suzanne would come and stay with him."

"So it was all about money with her."

"What else could it be. No one wants someone like Bart unless there's a promise of money."

Dirk and Brenda surveyed the damage from the storm.

"The house is ruined, and we don't have the funds to fix it," Brenda said. "I'm so glad Mother didn't have to see this."

"Well, we own half a ruined house. That's something, I guess."

"I suppose it is. The only thing we can do now is sell and buy something much, much smaller."

THANKSGIVING

Gwen and Allen Bates and their fifteen-year-old daughter, Lydia, were waiting in their living room for Gwen's brother, Bert, to drive them to Aunt Ettie's for Thanksgiving dinner.

Gwen glanced at the ornamental clock on the mantel. "Bert's always late. I don't know why we rushed to get ready." There was an awkward pause, then Gwen said, "While we wait, why don't we recount our blessings and say what we are thankful for this year. The rector said on Sunday that nobody knows how to be grateful anymore."

"Why don't you start then, Gwen," Allen said. "What are you thankful for this year?"

"That's easy," Gwen replied. "I'm thankful I don't have to cook a big Thanksgiving dinner. I wore myself out last year, and nothing really turned out right. This year, I'm bringing the deviled eggs and potato salad. That's about all I can handle."

Gwen turned toward Allen who was sitting on the gold damask easy chair near the large front window. "Now it's your turn, Al. What are you thankful for?"

"I'm thankful your brother is driving us to Aunt Ettie's in Glendora. I don't want anyone to see our Mazda until it's fixed. If your family sees that big dent in the passenger door, they'll start asking me questions, and I really don't want to discuss it."

Gwen turned toward Lydia who was seated beside her on the gold velvet Victorian couch. "Now it's your turn, Lydia. What are you thankful for? I hope you'll tell us that you're grateful you have such kind and thoughtful parents."

Lydia looked directly at her mother. "I'm thankful I'm not old."

"You're thankful you're not old! What is that supposed to mean?"

"It means exactly what I said. I'm thankful I'm not old. I don't want to be like Aunt Helen who has a painful hip and uses a cane. Besides, what man wants a fifty-year-old woman? Being young, I'm the center of attention."

"You're much too young to be thinking about boys," Gwen replied.

"That's true," Lydia said, "but I love it when they think about me."

"I'm sorry I even started this conversation," Gwen said. "I'm two years older than Helen. You must think I'm ready for my grave."

"All I said, Mother, is that I'm thankful I'm not old. What's wrong with that?"

"I was young and beautiful, too, Lydia. Don't forget that. And I remember Helen twenty-five years ago. She was a knockout. No wonder my brother married her."

"I don't care if other people are old," Lydia said, "but I'm glad I'm not one of them."

"That's such a shallow philosophy, Lydia. Someday you will be old too. You should look at old people with awe and reverence. Think of all the wonderful things they've done and the experiences they've had."

"I think you are taking this personally, Gwen," Allen said. "Lydia isn't criticizing you for being old. She wants to celebrate her youth and enjoy it. I see nothing wrong in that."

"I'm not old!" Gwen said loudly.

"You're not old compared to Aunt Ettie, but you're old compared to Lydia. Let's leave it at that."

A car horn honked. Gwen rose from the couch. "It's Bert. Let's go." Gwen looked at Lydia. "Don't you dare tell Helen she's old."

Lydia's voice was full of irony. "I will look at Aunt Helen with awe and reverence, just as you told me."

"I don't know why I have such an awful daughter," Gwen said.

"Leave Lydia alone," Allen replied. "I'm glad she's thankful for her youth. When it's gone, it's gone, and nothing can bring it back."

Becoming Famous

Abigail Van Brock stood before the easel in her studio. "I'm simply not inspired to do anything today."

"Why not, Abigail?"

"I don't know, Wendell. I feel like I've run out of steam."

"Is it because your paintings don't sell?"

"I guess that's part of it. I feel like I'm the Van Gogh of the twenty-first century, but I'm the only one who knows it."

"Maybe one Van Gogh is enough."

"One Van Gogh is never enough, but the world doesn't seem to know that."

"The walls of this studio are covered with your paintings, and you have so many stored away that haven't even been framed."

Abigail sighed. "This is my legacy to the world, but it is a legacy which no one wants."

"Many creative people create things which no one wants. Look at Charlie Hanschell. He's written ten novels, and no publisher wants them."

"And they're good too," Abigail added. "I've read three of them."

"Well, I like your paintings. This one you did of the house down the street is a masterpiece."

"Thank you, darling. It's nice to know I have one fan."

Standing in the doorway was the Van Brocks' daughter, Shirley. "You have two fans, Mother."

Abigail turned toward her daughter. "Oh Shirley, you're home from work. You and your father are such dears to love my paintings. At least I've made a hit with my family."

"You've made a hit with more than your family. I showed one of your paintings to my boss, and he wants to buy a hundred of them."

"A hundred! What could he possibly do with a hundred paintings?"

"Well, everyone who comes into the furniture store and buys a living-room suite will receive one of your paintings gratis. He feels it will be a great sales promotion gimmick."

"That's wonderful, Shirley. That means my paintings will be in living rooms all across California."

"Yes, and your name will be featured in all the advertisements. You will be described as one of America's most brilliant new artists. You will also be interviewed on radio in connection with the promotion. Gus has to promote you in order to promote his furniture."

Abigail's face beamed with happiness. "Oh, Shirley, I can't thank you enough for doing this for me. This is the fulfillment of a dream. Tell Gus I will let him have my paintings at a special reduced price of a thousand dollars each."

"A thousand dollars each! I had no idea you would want so much, Mother."

"Well, my regular price is two thousand dollars, so Gus is getting a tremendous discount."

"But you've never sold any of your paintings at any price."

"That doesn't matter. I put a tremendous amount of work into these paintings. Anything less than a thousand dollars would be a giveaway price. I'd sooner donate my paintings to charity than accept less."

"Mother, I've worked really hard to convince Gus to do this. I told him many famous artists have raved about your work. I know it's not true, but he'll never know the difference."

"How much does Gus plan to pay me then?"

"He only wanted to pay thirty dollars a painting, but I talked him into paying fifty based on your extraordinary talent and all the praise I said you've received from artists and art critics. That's five thousand dollars you would have in your pocket. It's a lot more than zero."

"Shirley, it would break my heart to let my paintings go for fifty dollars."

"Mother, think of all the promotion. Your name will be in all the newspaper ads, and you will be interviewed on radio."

"Talk to Gus again and see if you can't get a better price. Considering all the promotion I will receive, I will try to be flexible."

The next evening, Shirley found her mother seated in the kitchen drinking coffee. She poured herself a cup and sat down beside her.

"Did you talk to Gus?" Abigail asked.

"Yes, I did. He won't go above fifty dollars, but he'll throw in a five-thousand-dollar bonus if he sells a hundred living room suites in the next two months. That's a total of ten thousand dollars."

Abigail smiled. "It's not what my paintings are worth, but I've decided the promotion will be worth it. Tell Gus we have a deal."

Abigail Van Brock never received the ten thousand dollars because Gus's furniture store went out of business six months later, but the promotion made her famous. An art gallery in Beverly Hills sold the remaining fifty paintings Abigail had on hand at prices she had never dreamed of.

THE ONE-MAN SHOW

Alvin Huff was in his study when his son, Lester, came into the room.

"I hate to disturb you, Dad, while you're working on your computer, but I want to give you something."

Alvin turned away from the computer screen. "What is it, Les?"

"Please don't call me Les. I am now Chris Branagan."

"The name Les is on your birth certificate."

"It may be on my birth certificate, but Lester Huff is a nowhere name as far as acting is concerned."

"Okay, I'll just call you son. How's that?"

"Please call me Chris when other people are present. An actor's name is his trademark."

"Okay then, I'll call you Chris when other people are around. What is it you want?"

"I don't want anything. I want to give you something." Les handed his father a piece of paper. "This is a ticket to my one-man show on Friday night. I've already given Mother hers."

"This ticket is something you've printed on your computer. What sort of playhouse are we talking about?"

"Never mind that. I've written a one-man play. Everyone says it will launch my career."

Lester's mother, Mary Jane, entered the room. "Have you told your father about your play, Les—I mean, Chris?"

"Yes, but not the details."

"Oh, Al, Chris's play is wonderful, and when he performs it, he is so funny."

"Does he get paid for his performance?"

"Of course not. Don't be so materialistic."

Mary Jane turned toward her son. "Your father is one of those people who only thinks of money."

"Money is not the worst thing to think about," Alvin replied.

"It is when it corrodes your soul," Mary Jane said. "Chris is creative. He is brilliant. I would never condemn him to work at an ordinary job."

"Why is it that I have two clever daughters and a son who merely wants to be an unpaid actor?" Alvin asked.

"Susan is a pharmacist, and Cecelia is an accountant," Mary Jane replied. "Those jobs pay well."

"Then why can't Lester be a pharmacist or an accountant and make a decent salary?"

"Because those jobs don't interest him," Mary Jane replied.

"I wasted all that money, hoping Les would go on to law school," Alvin said, "but he flunked out in his junior year."

"Let's not have recriminations," Mary Jane said. "When you see Chris's performance Friday night, you will be thrilled."

Chris's one-man show on Friday was at a small theater near Hollywood that seated thirty people. Every seat was taken, and there were several people who were forced to stand.

"There's nothing like a crowd," Mary Jane said to Alvin after the performance was over, and they were walking toward their car.

"Thirty-five people is not a crowd."

"It is in a small theater."

"I didn't like the nudity," Alvin said.

"Chris had to get the audience's attention somehow."

"I never thought I would have a son who wanted to be a porn star."

"That wasn't pornography. That was humor."

"I didn't like the vulgar language either."

"The language was shocking," Mary Jane replied, "but if Chris hadn't used it, he would have disappointed his audience."

Alvin and Mary Jane were seated in their living room when Lester entered the house later that evening. He was accompanied by a young woman he introduced as Wendy.

"Guess what, Dad? Wendy's mother was so impressed by my performance tonight she is going to fund my next play providing her daughter is given a starring role."

"I hope there will be no nudity," Alvin said.

"Wendy will be fully clothed, and I will be dressed above the waist."

"What is it about?"

"It's about the love of a President for his intern."

"That should be wonderful," Mary Jane exclaimed. "I love movies and plays that deal with history."

THE BACHELOR

Helen was sitting in the study crocheting an afghan, when Allen entered the room. "Allen, sit down. There's something I want to talk to you about."

Allen sat down in the burgundy wing chair. "What is it Helen?"

"I think we should alter our will."

"Alter our will! Why should we do that?"

"It's Raymond. I'm worried about him."

"Worried?"

"Yes, worried. Etta telephoned me this afternoon. She's such a lovely girl, but she's very unhappy."

"Why is that?"

"Raymond won't marry her. They've been living together for over a year, and she feels she's just wasting her time with him."

"Well, that's not our problem."

"Yes, it is our problem. Raymond should settle down. He's lived with five different women and always refuses to marry them. I think we should change our will to read that if he doesn't marry by the time he's forty-five, everything should go to Harry."

"Harry's our adopted son."

"That doesn't matter. He's devoted to his wife and has five beautiful children."

"I can't imagine you saying this, Helen. Why would you want to cheat Raymond out of his inheritance?"

"I'm not cheating him out of his inheritance. He's thirty-five now, so that gives him ten years to get married. He doesn't have to marry Etta, even though she would be a perfect wife for him, but he does have to marry someone."

"I will not alter the will," Allen said.

"Okay then, you don't have to alter the will. I will simply tell Raymond that we've made a new will. That will pressure him to marry Etta. He won't know how the will actually reads until one of us dies."

"I think this is a mistake, Helen. Raymond has to live his own life, not ours."

"I'm doing this for Raymond's own good."

Six months later, Helen met Allen at the front door of the house.

"Allen, I have the most wonderful news. Raymond's married!"

"Married!"

"Yes, married! I received a telephone call from Raymond this afternoon. He and his new bride eloped to Hawaii, and they're now back in Los Angeles. He's moved into her home in Brentwood and renting out his condo."

"What happened to Etta?"

"I didn't ask, but she must have disappeared somewhere along the way. We have an invitation to meet the beautiful new bride this evening."

"Is she beautiful?"

"I'm sure she must be. Raymond wouldn't settle for anything less."

That evening, Allen and Helen drove out to Brentwood to meet Raymond and his new wife, Alexandra. They were immediately impressed by the large size of the house. It was a white Spanish-style two-story home with a traditional red-tile roof.

"What a splendid house," Helen said. "I'm surprised a young girl would have this kind of money."

Helen rang the doorbell. A gray-haired lady with a cane answered the door.

"Would you tell Alexandra we're here. We're expected. Let her know we're Raymond's parents."

In a firm voice, the lady said, "I am Alexandra."

"You are?"

"Who else would I be?"

Alexandra led Helen and Allen into the large living room. They sat down on the blue damask couch. Alexandra seated herself beside Raymond on a matching loveseat.

"My maid will bring in tea in a few minutes," Alexandra said. "Meanwhile, let me tell you how much I adore your son." She cuddled up to Raymond. "I especially adore his huge brick-layer arms."

Helen seemed at a loss for words. Finally, she said in a weak voice, "I'm glad you're happy."

"Raymond's my toy boy," Alexandra said. "Although I'm a few years older than he is, I don't think that will be a problem. My previous husband was forty years older than me, and we were very happy. He died last year at one hundred years young."

"You're a widow then," Helen said.

"Yes, of course. The whole thing was very sad at the end, but Vince and I had ten wonderful years together. Vince had five children from previous marriages, but he left everything to me. He said I was the only woman who ever made him completely happy. I know Raymond will feel the same way."

Alexandra chatted on. Helen was mostly quiet. She didn't look happy.

When Alexandra left the room, Raymond said, "Mother, I owe all this to you. I would never have gotten married if you hadn't changed your will. Alexandra has had six previous husbands, and I feel very lucky to be number seven."

Helen smiled weakly, but said nothing.

When Allen and Helen left Alexandra's home that evening, Allen said in a voice that was heavy with irony, "You got your wish, Helen. Raymond did exactly what you wanted him to do. He got married. So smile and be happy."

Helen didn't answer, nor did she say anything during the drive home.

THE BIG DEAL

"This is a big deal, a very big deal," Alice Firwood said as she sat on the red velvet easy chair in her living room. "In fact, this deal is what I've been waiting for all my life."

Alex Firwood was sitting opposite his wife on a matching red velvet couch. "How can you say that, Alice? You'll just lose a lot of money, and nothing will happen."

"I don't agree, and you're not going to talk me out of it. I get to play the part of Julie. It's a tremendous role. I've read the script, and I love it."

"But you have so little acting experience."

"Nonsense. I've been in several plays. They weren't big roles, but everyone could see my potential."

"Those were plays at City College. That was a long time ago."

"Fifteen years is not a long time."

"The part I don't like is that you have to invest $100,000 in order to appear in the film."

"Gertrude is starting a little independent film company," Alice replied. "She has to raise the capital somehow. She offered me the part of Cynthia if I could put up $200,000, but I figured $100,000 was my limit."

"It's the money you inherited from your father, so I can't tell you how to spend it, but I think you're making a mistake."

"When you see my name in lights on Hollywood Boulevard, you'll change your tune."

Alice didn't speak much about the film after that, and Alex put the whole thing out of his mind.

A year later, on the night of the premiere at Gertrude's house, Alex escorted Alice in a rented tuxedo. Alice looked radiant in her evening dress. There were about thirty people present for the viewing. The provocative title of the film was *Sowing Wild Oats*.

"Wasn't I wonderful?" Alice asked after the movie was over.

"You were," Alex replied but without enthusiasm.

"I think this will open doors for me," Alice said.

"It might," Alex replied.

Alice never appeared in one of Gertrude's films again because she didn't want to give her another $100,000, but she showed a DVD of the film to friends whenever they came over. Everyone politely agreed she had a lot of talent.

One night, Alice and Alex were watching a television documentary. It was entitled *The Worst Films Ever Made*. There were excerpts from *Sowing Wild Oats*. The announcer predicted that when the movie became better known, it would become a cult classic. The actors were clumsy, wooden, and lifeless; but in a way, the movie was hilarious. The actors had unwittingly turned a drama into a comedy. Carol Burnett couldn't have done it better. Laugh tracks were inserted when the movie excerpts were shown, which made Alex laugh when he hadn't dared laugh before.

After the documentary was over, Alice said, "I told you I was a great actress. Nobody knew I could do comedy, but I knew it all along. And you tried to discourage me, Alex. Shame on you. I'm glad I never listened."

FISHING

Carol Harworth was working her tablet in the den when she put it on a side table and looked across the room at Jason Harworth who was seated in an easy chair reading a financial magazine.

"You know, Jason, I'm getting a little annoyed with Sheila."

Jason looked up from his magazine. "Annoyed with Sheila? I thought you two were best friends."

"We are, but lately she's started fishing."

"Fishing?"

"Yes, you know the system where people ask you subtle but leading questions, hoping to trip you up and get you to reveal things that are none of their business."

"That sounds like you with me."

"Nonsense, I never fish."

"You do all the time, but never mind that. What is Sheila trying to get you to reveal?"

"She seems to want to know about our love life."

"I hope you told her I'm a rocket in bed."

"Why would you want me to lie?"

"I don't want you to lie, but you might exaggerate a little."

"It seems Sheila and Ben haven't done anything much since their honeymoon," Carol said.

"Ben doesn't look like a high-energy person," Jason replied, "so in a way I'm not surprised. But how did they get five children?"

"Sheila said something about a fertility clinic. I didn't want to press her for details."

"We must be boring people."

"Why?"

"Because we got our children the old-fashioned way."

Jason looked up and saw their eighteen-year-old daughter, Etta, in the doorway of the den.

"What are you two talking about?"

"Nothing much," Carol said.

"That's not true. You're hiding something from me."

"No, we're not," Carol replied.

"Yes, you are. I heard something about an old-fashioned fertility clinic. Are you saying you're not my parents?"

"Of course we're your parents."

"Why are my eyes blue then, when you both have brown eyes?"

"Stop this," Carol said. "You're out of control."

"I have a right to know if I was adopted," Etta said.

"This has nothing to do with you."

"If I'm adopted, it has everything to do with me. I'll tell Sharon we're adopted as soon as she gets home."

"Leave your sister out of this."

"Mother, why do you do this to me? I'm tired of your lies."

"Don't you dare speak to me that way."

"If you're not my mother, I'll speak to you any way I want to."

"I don't know why I ever had children."

"Etta, stop fishing," Jason said. "We'll tell you the whole story if you promise to keep it a secret."

"Of course, I'll keep it a secret."

"Your mother was telling me that Sheila's children are the product of a fertility clinic."

"Oh really. That's interesting. No wonder they look the way they do."

"Remember, keep it a secret," Jason said.

"No, this is something I could never keep secret. Children have a right to know who their real parents are."

"Etta, you're being a troublemaker," Jason said.

"No, I'm not. I don't believe in lies."

"Poor Sheila," Carol said. "Now it's going to be all over the neighborhood, but if she hadn't started fishing, I would never have told a soul."

HARRY

Gerald's happiest day was when his son was born. After having four daughters that he couldn't really afford, his son was like the icing on the cake.

"I think we have enough children now," Marcia said to Gerald after Harry was born. "We live in this cramped house, and the noise from the children is sometimes deafening."

"You wanted a large family, and so did I. We got our wish, so don't complain now."

"Watch well thy wish lest it fill thy dish," Marcia said

"My grandmother said that all the time, but I don't think it applies in our case. Harry will make a mark in the world and make us proud. He looks like a wrestler."

"He's only a month old. How can you tell?"

"Look at those arms."

"All babies have arms like that."

"Well, look at those feet. He'll make John Wayne look like a sissy."

"John Wayne had very small feet."

"I didn't know that, but Harry's stare will intimidate anyone. I'd hate to meet him in a dark alley."

"Gerald, do you want a son or do you want a monster?"

"I guess I want a son to be all the things I'm not."

"Well, you're not a wrestler, and you're not John Wayne, but I love you anyway. I'm not sure I want a son who's a monster."

"We'll start Harry on the right track, Marcia. We'll give him boxing lessons and pay for his membership in a gym. He'll play football in high school, and we'll go to every game."

"I don't want a son who plays football, Gerald. He could be hurt."

"Not Harry. He's much too tough."

"Harry's only a month old!"

"I can see it in Harry's eyes, Marcia. He's got the eyes of a killer."

"Gerald, shut up! Harry's just a baby! I'll teach him to write poetry and play the violin. Boys need to develop their sensitive side."

"Not Harry. He doesn't have a sensitive side, and he's definitely not playing the violin."

But as Harry grew up, Gerald grew disillusioned. Harry was not athletic and didn't want to play football. He didn't even want to play ping-pong or shuffleboard. In Gerald's eyes, Harry was a failure.

Marcia, on the other hand, decided not to teach Harry poetry. He couldn't spell. He could barely even read. But Marcia insisted Harry play the violin. She made him practice two hours every day until the violin teacher told her Harry had no musical ability. Marcia realized she was wasting her money and stopped the lessons.

But Harry's biggest sin in Marcia's eyes was that he was embarrassingly fat. People would say, "Is that fat boy your son?" Marcia would pretend she didn't hear. That sort of remark didn't deserve an answer.

Instead of talking about Harry, Gerald and Marcia praised their daughters endlessly. All of them had promising careers in law, accounting, and teaching.

Harry became invisible.

While their daughters moved out of the family one by one, Harry stayed at home. He couldn't seem to hold a job. Everything would be fine for a few weeks, and then he would be terminated for reasons that varied: Sometimes he couldn't do the work, sometimes he wouldn't do the work, and sometimes he didn't show up for work. Harry complained of migraine headaches and suffered from constant colds. Gerald and Marcia realized Harry would have to stay with them for the rest of their lives. If they asked Harry to leave, he would be homeless, and they didn't want that.

However, when Harry was twenty-five, he won the lottery. Without telling his parents, he went to a realtor and bought a mansion. It was on three acres of ground with large statues of Marcellus, Jupiter, Venus, Hercules, Pan, Mars, Minerva, and Hebe on either side of the entry walk. The house was massive and looked like it had been transported to California from ancient Rome. One expected the Emperor Hadrian to appear in the doorway at any moment.

When Marcia and Gerald walked up the grand staircase to the second floor and roamed through the fifty rooms of the house, they had trouble believing such a magnificent mansion existed. It must all surely be a dream.

"I guess you'll be leaving us," Marcia said to Harry.

"No, this is your house Mom as well as Dad's. I put both your names on the deed as well as mine. You can use your old house as a rental so you won't have to work."

"Harry, this is the most wonderful thing that has ever happened to me."

Gerald smiled. "We knew Harry was special all along, didn't we, Marcia?"

"Of course we did. We couldn't have wanted a better son," Marcia replied.

Suddenly Harry didn't seem to be overweight to Marcia, and Gerald taught Harry to swim in the large pool. Perhaps ping-pong and shuffleboard were out of his league, but he could swim.

"Harry is the perfect son," Marcia said to Gerald again when Harry was out of earshot. "We couldn't have wanted him to be anything more."

"I totally agree," Gerald replied. "I totally agree."

It Walked into a Bar

Arlette entered the house and saw her father, Rick Hartwood, sitting on the living-room couch beside a small white dog.

"Where in the world did you get that cute little white dog?"

Rick smiled. "It walked into a bar and said, 'I want you to take me home.'"

"Don't tease me, Dad. Tell me the truth."

"That is the truth. The dog entered the bar. I was sitting in a booth all alone. The dog came up to me wagging its tail. I gave him some of my sandwich. The rest is history."

"But who does the dog belong to? You can't just pick up someone's dog and take him home."

"The dog belonged to the bartender. He said it was a toy poodle. I gave him a hundred dollars."

"Does he have a name?" Arlette asked.

"I'm calling him Ramses."

"Ramses! That's not a very good name for something so small and cute. I think you should call him Lovems."

"Lovems! How can he lead an army with a name like Lovems?"

"Stop it, Dad! Lovems is not going to lead an army."

"Well, he might be confronted by a pack of wild dogs. They would never respect someone called Lovems."

"He's Lovems as far as I'm concerned," Arlette replied. "May I pick him up?"

"Of course."

Arlette picked up Lovems and cuddled him in her arms. "He's just adorable, Dad. I feel like I'm holding a baby."

Rick smiled. "Don't have any babies until you're thirty. They're too much trouble."

Arlette pretended to pout and spoke in a high squeaky voice, "Was I too much trouble?"

"You cried a lot, Arlette. We were up all night."

"Well, Lovems will never be any trouble, Dad. I'll look after him and feed him. He can sleep with me at night."

"It seems I've just lost a dog."

"You may have lost a dog," Arlette replied, "but I've gained the most adorable little baby in the world."

While Arlette was sitting in an easy chair cuddling Lovems, her mother, Harriette, entered the house.

"What on earth is that animal doing in here?"

"Animal!" Arlette exclaimed. "This is not an animal. This is Lovems."

"Well, take that animal outside. He'll chew on the upholstery and shed fur. I don't want my beautiful new furniture ruined. How many people have an expensive red velvet Victorian living-room suite?"

"Lovems is my baby," Arlette said.

"That is not a baby. That is a dog," Harriette said. "It goes outside."

"Dad, stand up for me," Arlette said.

"I hadn't thought about the dog ruining the furniture," Rick replied. "We can buy a dog house and keep him outside."

"Not Lovems! Lovems is my baby."

"Lovems is not a baby," Harriette said. "Get it outside before it does something awful on my magnificent Oriental rug."

Arlette gave her mother a look of disgust and took Lovems into her bedroom.

Twenty minutes later, Arlette returned to the living room without Lovems.

"I'm moving out," Arlette said.

"Moving out!" Harriette exclaimed. "How can you be moving out? You're only fifteen?"

"I telephoned Granny Hartwood. She says Lovems and I are both welcome in her home. She will pick me up tonight."

"How could you do this to me, Arlette? You know Granny Hartwood and I don't get along. She doesn't care about you or the dog. She just wants to spite me."

"Granny says you put on airs, Mother, and I believe her."

"I do not put on airs," Harriette replied angrily. "I never put on airs. Granny Hartwood lives in a trailer. What would she know about putting on airs?"

"Well, all I can say is that Lovems and I are going to live with Granny."

The next day at breakfast, Harriette sat opposite Rick at the small wooden table on the far side of the kitchen near the bright, sunny window. As she poured cornflakes into a bowl, she said, "I hate your mother for doing this to me. She has no right to turn Arlette against me."

"Mother hasn't done anything wrong," Rick replied.

"Well, she'll have to look after Arlette at her own expense. I'm not giving your mother a penny for Arlette's keep."

"Being angry and bitter never helped anyone."

"She was such an adorable little girl, but now she's growing up and has no use for her mother, and it all happened because of a dog."

"Someday you'll be friends again," Rick replied. "Just give it a little time. As Arlette gets a little older, she'll come to realize just how much you love her."

A Feeling of Satisfaction

Gerald's wife loved to acquire things, almost anything. Their small house was jammed with everything from fine antiques to glassware from the 99-Cent Store.

"Why do you do this, Mildred? Why can't you stop buying things? Our house looks like a museum. I feel like I'm living in a warehouse, not a home."

"Gerald, you just don't understand me. When I see certain things, I just have to have them. I can't rest until I possess them, and then, once I make my purchase, I have the most wonderful feeling of satisfaction. It's better than making love. I feel complete and whole and wonderful."

"Last week you bought that dinner service for six, and you've never even looked at it. It's still setting in a box in the music room, unpacked. Why on earth did you buy it?"

"Gerald, you are totally uncivilized, a hopeless barbarian. That is not just a complete dinner service for six. It's a Wedgwood bone china dinner service for six in the Osborne pattern. Do you know how much I have longed to possess a Wedgwood bone china dinner service in the Osborne pattern? And now, I finally have a complete set. It's one of the most wonderful things to have happened to me."

"You have so much Wedgwood, Mildred, and you never look at it or use it."

"One can never have too much Wedgwood."

Gerald went into the music room to read his newspaper. On his right side was a tall bookcase jammed with some of Mildred's massive collection of books. On his left side were the tall cases that contained Mildred's massive collection of videos. They were rarely watched anymore. Mildred was busy buying DVDs which were kept in cases in the back bedroom.

Gerald was a pudgy, balding man of forty-five. Seated in a wicker easy chair between the books and the videos, he felt intimidated by Mildred's possessions. They made him feel insignificant. Mildred's real lovers were her things, things she only cared about until she acquired them. He had been pursued and acquired too, and now he sat in a wicker chair, looking across the room at a massive china cabinet that was crammed with porcelain and crystal, which prevented him from seeing out the music-room window.

Mildred was forty and still attractive. She was always carefully dressed when she went out. Her clothes were carefully selected to enhance her ladylike image. She was never sloppy or casual. But with fifty handbags and a hundred pairs of shoes and endless dresses, blouses, and suits, she rarely appeared in the same outfit twice in the same year.

Mildred could be very witty and had a delightful sense of humor. When she was in the right mood, she could be the center of attention. Gerald was always proud to be her escort, and Mildred always made certain he was dressed properly when they went out together. She usually selected his clothes, which he appreciated, since it prevented him from making a mistake.

While Gerald was seated in the wicker chair, Mildred entered the music room. "Did you say you were going to San Francisco next week?"

"Yes. It's the business trip I told you about. I'll be gone from Monday till Friday. Will you miss me?"

"Of course, I'll miss you. You're the most important thing I own, but there'll be a big surprise for you when you come back."

"I guess you'll have some cleaning people come in. Hasn't it been about two or three months?"

"You'll see."

Gerald always let Mildred attend to the household chores, and she wouldn't have it any other way. Careless hands could break things. That was more responsibility than he wanted to handle.

A week later, when Gerald returned from San Francisco, all the lights in the house were off. He had expected Mildred to be there to greet him, but she wasn't. Gerald switched on the living room light. What a shock! Almost all the furniture was gone. They had been robbed!

Gerald went through the house. The TV was still there. Mildred's clothes were still in their bedroom. The bed was there. The kitchen, music room, back bedroom, and living room were almost all empty. Who would steal all the porcelain and crystal? Who would want it?

Gerald picked up the phone to call the police and then put it down. Mildred was probably at the police station now reporting the crime. No wonder she was not at home. He would just have to wait until she returned.

A half hour later, Gerald heard Mildred's car pull into the driveway. He went out onto the porch. "I guess you've been at the police station."

"Police station? What for?"

"To report the crime."

"What crime?"

"We've been robbed. The house is almost empty. Didn't you know?"

Mildred smiled as they entered the living room. "I've put everything in storage, Gerald."

"But why? There's not even a microwave in the kitchen."

"As you know, Aunt Sally died and left everything to her daughter, Sharon. Sharon's selling her Glendale house and moving into Aunt Sally's place in San Marino, but she already has more furniture and china than she needs, so she's letting me have all Aunt Sally's things. She is thrilled that her mother's things will be kept in the family. The movers will be bringing it here next week. I've always wanted a grandfather clock and a Tiffany glass lamp. Aunt Sally had such exquisite taste. You can't imagine the treasures we will have. It will be a whole new look."

Mildred glanced approvingly at the empty rooms. "Any time I want some of my old treasures back, I can retrieve them from storage, but I won't do that for a while. The prospect of having all the wonderful things Aunt Sally had gives me such a wonderful feeling of satisfaction. It's like making love, only much, much better."

A HALLOWEEN TALE

Grezinka the witch had long stringy hair, a large bulbous nose, crooked teeth, and a weak chin. When the sun set at the beginning of Halloween, she pushed open her coffin, shoved her gravestone away, and climbed out of her grave with her black broomstick. Beside her, was her black cat, Shackles.

"Shackles, am I not the most beautiful woman you have ever seen?"

Shackles did not reply.

"Well, I will be, Shackles, if I can stay alive until midnight and kiss one of the saints who comes out on All Saints' Day. It says so in my book on magic. The saint will shrivel into nothingness as I suck the life out of him, but what is that to me? The world would be a better place if there were fewer saints and more devils."

"Harry, are you telling the children that horrible story about Grezinka the witch?"

"I am, Beverly, by popular demand."

"I want to hear the story, Mommy," Breanna said. "I love the part where the dragon tries to stop Grezinka from kissing a saint, but Shackles turns into a huge snake and swallows the dragon."

"But then the dragon breathes fire inside the snake's stomach," Jimmy said, "and makes the snake sick, so the dragon leaves the snake's stomach, and the snake turns back into Shackles."

"And then the witch goes into the castle on top of the mountain," Breanna continued, "and Shackles turns into a lion and corners a handsome prince so the witch can kiss him, but the prince is not a saint, so he turns into a lizard and Shackles eats him."

"Really Harry, I don't know why you persist in telling the children such an awful story."

"Halloween comes but once a year, and whether we like it or not, it is about ghosts and ghouls and even witches."

"Well, I stopped at the store today and bought Breanna a beautiful princess costume for the Halloween party at Aunt Sarah's. I will make her so pretty she will look like a china doll."

Breanna made a face. "Mother, a princess! I don't want to be a princess! I want to be a witch like Grezinka."

"And then, I bought a crown, a robe, and sandals for Jimmy so he can dress as King Lear."

"I want to be a black cat like Shackles," Jimmy said, "so I can turn into a snake and eat the dragon."

"I don't want any arguments," Beverly said. "I paid good money for your costumes, and you're wearing them whether you like it or not."

"Mother, you're no fun," Jimmy said.

"Princesses are just plain boring," Breanna added.

"Well, I want you to be ready to leave with your father for Aunt Sarah's by five thirty. I'm going to stop at the deli and pick up the food. I'm transferring it to my dishes so Sarah will think I made it myself. I hope the three of you are clever enough to keep my secret."

Harry and the children left for the party at five thirty, and Beverly went to the deli and purchased the food she thought would most easily pass for homemade. Then she went home and put the Caesar salad, the three-bean salad, and the sausages in antique covered porcelain bowls, each of which had three feet and was hand-painted and trimmed in gold.

When Beverly arrived at the party, she put the three antique covered bowls on her sister-in-law Sarah's buffet.

"Beverly, where on earth did you find such magnificent bowls?"

Beverly believed strict accuracy was never necessary when discussing antiques. "I found them in a little shop just off Rodeo Drive."

"They're exquisite. You must have paid a fortune for them." Sarah lifted the cover off one of the bowls. "Three-bean salad, my favorite. I have a confession to make, Beverly. I didn't have time to cook, so I picked up some food at the deli. It won't be anything like your delicious fare, but I simply ran out of time."

While they were talking, a little girl in a black ankle-length dress and cape and a black cone-shaped hat came into the room. There was a hideous mask over her face. "Hee, hee, hee! I'm Grezinka the witch."

"Breanna is that you? What on earth happened to your princess costume?" Beverly asked.

Sarah answered for Breanna. "It was one of those terrible accidents. Breanna wanted some punch, but somehow the punch bowl tipped over, and the punch stained her beautiful princess costume. She didn't want to wear the princess costume Lydia wore last year, so I let her wear the witch outfit Alice wore three years ago."

"Hee, hee, hee! I'm Grezinka the witch!" Breanna chanted as she walked about the room. "Hee, hee, hee! I'm Grezinka the witch!"

THE CHAIR

Phillip was seated on the gold, velvet Chippendale couch in his living room, looking at a dull brown easy chair on the other side of the room. "Monica, don't you think we should do something about that chair?"

"Chair? You mean Mother's chair?"

"It's so dull and worn, and there's that rip in the upholstery."

"That chair is not to be touched. Mother sat in that chair the last twenty years before she died. It's the only thing I have left of her."

"Wouldn't it be better to have it reupholstered?"

"Absolutely not. Mother could hardly walk. She sat in that chair all day long and crocheted those beautiful afghans with the red roses. Even now I see her sitting in that chair working her crochet hook."

"Perhaps we should move on."

"Move on, Phil! What sort of talk is that! As long as I'm alive, Mother will never be forgotten. I'm not like Evelyn. She's not sentimental at all. Evelyn has never visited Mother's grave, and she lives only six miles from Eureka."

"We've been driving up there every three or four months, and it's over seven hundred miles."

"That's what I mean, Phil. We're dedicated to Mother, Evelyn isn't."

"Not to change the subject, but did you remember to telephone Evelyn and ask her to house-sit for us while we're in Europe?"

"I did, and she was thrilled. She's always wanted to see Los Angeles. She's going to do all the tourist things: visit the Huntington

Galleries, the art museum on Wilshire Boulevard as well as Exposition Park. She even wants to ride Angels Flight."

"Will she need your car?"

"Yes, she will. She doesn't like the idea of the long drive down here, so she's going to fly."

"Well, I feel good about having a house sitter while we're gone," Phil said. "These houses are broken into all the time."

Phillip and Monica had a wonderful time in Europe. They visited fifteen countries in fourteen days. Although they didn't remember much about any particular country, they remembered a little about each. Monica remembered there was an impressive tower in Paris, but she couldn't recall its name. Phillip learned that the Vatican was in Italy. Someone had told him once that it was in Spain. They both agreed that travel had broadened their horizons.

As Phillip and Monica went up the front steps of their house, Evelyn opened the front door to greet them. "How are the happy travelers?"

"Very happy," Phil said. "We never knew Europe could be so interesting."

"I'll have to go sometime. Ed doesn't like to travel so I'll have to go alone, I suppose."

As Phillip and Monica set their bags down in the entry hall, Evelyn said, "I have some coffee on. Why don't you two go into the living room, and I'll bring you a cup?"

But when Monica went into the living room, she was astonished. She yelled in a loud voice, "Evelyn, where is Mother's chair?"

Evelyn walked calmly into the living room, carrying three cups of coffee and some tea biscuits on a tray. She set the tray down on the coffee table. "Try to compose yourself, Monica. You've been obsessing about Mother for far too long. Mother is dead, and she's not coming back. In case you didn't know, dead is spelled D-E-A-D. It's complete, final, and absolute."

"I didn't ask for a lecture," Monica replied. "I asked where you put Mother's chair."

"In order to protect your sanity, Monica, I gave that ragged, worthless chair to the Goodwill. I'm surprised they even took it."

"How could you do that, Evelyn! I must ask you to leave my house as soon as you possibly can. When I write my will, I'll be sure you receive nothing."

Then Monica left the house.

Evelyn explained to Phillip how she only had Monica's best interests at heart, but she wouldn't stay another night. She called a taxi and went to a hotel.

Three hours later, Monica returned to the house. "Phillip, help me carry Mother's chair into the living room."

"You found the chair?"

"Yes, the man at the Goodwill was so kind. It was a miracle the chair was still there. We had to look everywhere."

When Phillip and Monica were seated again in the living room, Monica said, "Mother helped me find that chair. I know she did. It's all I have left of her. People can laugh about ghosts and spirits, but they're real. Mother helped me find that chair, and I will never let it go."

FAKE NEWS

"I don't know why I bother having everyone over for Thanksgiving. It's nothing but trouble and complaints."

Jake was seated in the burgundy wing chair in front of the sunny front window in the living room. He always knew when Betty was present because of the heavy fragrance of her perfume. Jake looked up from his book. "What's the matter now, Betty?"

Betty sat near Jake on the gold French provincial couch. "It's that stupid sister of yours. She complained the turkey I cooked was too dry. Too dry! How could it be too dry!"

"Isabel's a troublemaker. You know that. She's always been difficult."

"And all she brought was potato salad. She claims she made it herself, but I know better. It tastes exactly like the potato salad at Vons Deli."

"Well, at least Leslie's having everyone over for Christmas, so Isabel can run her down instead of you."

"Leslie's making a big mistake by taking on Christmas. It's too much work, and she's really not up to it."

"If I know Leslie, she'll have a deli cook everything. That's probably what you should do."

"Why should I? I love to cook, but when I work that hard over a dinner, I don't like someone ripping me to shreds."

At that moment, Sadie entered the living room. "I hear loud voices. Is something wrong?"

"It's your Aunt Isabel, Sadie. She's picking on me. She complained the Thanksgiving turkey was too dry. I don't know why

I bother having everyone over for the holidays when all I get are complaints."

Sadie sat down on the couch beside her mother. "I wouldn't worry about Aunt Isabel. The turkey was perfect, and your pumpkin pie was out of this world. Sharon tells me Uncle Chet complains about Aunt Isabel's cooking all the time, so I'm not surprised she's taking it out on you."

There was silence for a few moments, then Sadie said, "I would like to tell you something, but you must promise me you'll keep it a secret."

"You can tell your mother anything, Sadie. You know that."

"Nothing will go farther than this room," Jake said.

"Well, Sharon's very upset. She made me promise not to tell anyone."

"You should never have secrets from your mother," Betty said.

Sadie hesitated for a moment before speaking. "It seems Uncle Chet is having an affair."

"That sly old devil," Jake said.

Betty's voice was full of irritation. "Sly old devil! What kind of talk is that, Jake! This is about your sister!"

"I thought you didn't like her."

"I don't, but I don't want her marriage ruined. Think of our nieces and nephew."

"The worst part of it is the girl is only eighteen and still in high school," Sadie continued.

"I hate this sort of thing," Betty replied. "Why do middle-aged men have to pick on young girls?"

"Would it be better if Chet picked on an old lady?" Jake asked.

Betty glanced at Jake darkly. "You men always stick together."

There was silence for a few minutes, then Betty said, "I'm going to call Isabel and have a talk with her. She's got to nip this in the bud and clamp down on Chet hard."

"Mother, this is a secret. Sharon will never speak to me again or trust me if she knows I told you."

"Well, I would never tell her I heard it from you. Give me a little credit, please. I'll simply say I was visiting a friend near the high school and saw a student get in Chet's car."

"Mother! That's so transparent! Sharon will know right away that I told you."

"No, she won't. How could she? If I saw a high-school student get in Chet's car, what does that have to do with you?"

Betty said nothing about Uncle Chet at dinner that night as the family ate the leftovers from the Thanksgiving dinner, but when the dinner was over, Sadie said, "I suppose you've ruined my life, Mother."

"Ruined your life? What do you mean?"

"I'm sure you must have told Aunt Isabel about Uncle Chet by now."

There was a look of exasperation on Betty's face. "One thing I'm learning about people is you can't help them. I told Isabel I saw a beautiful blonde high-school girl climb into Chet's car and start necking with him. To make it realistic and to prove I was an eye witness, I gave Isabel a detailed report on the girl's physical appearance and how she was dressed. Isabel seemed stunned for a moment. Then after a long pause, she called me a liar and hung up. I don't know why I bother trying to help people. It's just not worth it."

"I don't think you have to worry about Isabel critiquing your turkey next Thanksgiving," Jake said. "I doubt if she'll show up."

"It's a thankless world," Betty replied, "a thankless world. I tried my best to help Isabel. I don't know why I bothered."

FORGIVENESS

Jake heard the front door open. He looked up from the book he was reading in the burgundy wing chair near the front window. "You're home early from church, Betty."

"I'm not in a good mood, Jake. The rector gave one of his silly sermons on forgiveness, and I wasn't in the mood to hear it, so I skipped the social hour and came right home."

"Forgiveness is one of the important principles of the Church."

Betty sat down on the gold French Provincial couch. "I suppose it is, but Father Goode really overdoes it. He's such a mealymouth."

"Maybe you should switch churches."

"I just might, if our dear minister doesn't stop trying to turn us into doormats."

"You're still mad about the will, aren't you?"

"Yes, and I don't intend to forgive anybody. Why should I? I was cheated out of a two-million-dollar house."

"You still got the cash."

"Yes, but I wanted the house."

"And the cash," Jake said.

"And the cash," Betty replied.

"Sharon was homeless, so your mother really had to take her in," Jake said. "It wouldn't have been right to let her continue sleeping in the streets."

"And it wasn't right for Sharon to cheat me out of the house," Betty replied. "I loved that house. I was raised there. The balcony had such a wonderful view of downtown. We could be enjoying that balcony now, watching the sun come up in the morning. I've never

54

liked this house ever since they built that apartment building next door and shut out the sunlight."

"Why do you think your mother left her house to Sharon?"

"Mother was tired of hearing Sharon's constant whining about being all alone and being forced out on the streets by me, the evil Betty, if I got the house. If I had known about the will, I would have torn it up, but I never suspected mother would have favored a niece over her own daughter."

"That is odd," Jake said. "You and your mother were always so close."

"Not close enough, apparently, to prevent Mother from being brainwashed by a lazy woman who has never worked a day in her life if she could help it. At times, I feel like burning Mother's house down, and if Sharon died in the flames, that would be a bonus."

"You don't have to forgive anyone Betty, but maybe you should forget about the house for a while. This thing will tear you up."

At that moment, Evelyn opened the front door and entered the living room.

"Mother, why didn't you want to stay for the social hour? Everyone asked after you."

"It's that silly rector and his stupid sermon. I just can't abide that man."

"Oh, but the sermon was so inspirational. I've already forgiven seven people."

"Well, as long as you haven't forgiven Sharon Sedgwick, I suppose it's okay."

Evelyn sat down beside her mother on the couch. "I went over to see Sharon yesterday afternoon. The house is already falling into ruin. Sharon has three men living with her. There are empty beer bottles everywhere. When one of them grabbed at me, I left."

Betty looked up at the ceiling and screamed to her dead mother, "Mother, how could you do this to me, your only daughter!"

Evelyn spoke, "The refreshments at the social hour were skimpy, and the coffee tasted like mud. Why don't I fix the three of us some bagels and cream cheese? Everyone's nerves are on edge when they're hungry."

Betty fell into a slump when Evelyn left the room. She let her head fall onto her breast and supported it with her left hand. Her depression emanated from her like rays of darkness.

After a long interval, Evelyn returned with toasted bagels and cream cheese and coffee served in bone china mugs covered with flowers. She placed her father's portion on a small table near him, and the rest she placed on the coffee table in front of the couch.

Betty raised her head. "How did you know I was hungry?"

"You skipped breakfast, so you had to be hungry."

"I'm not forgiving anybody."

"You don't have to. Bitterness is wonderful. Hold on to it as long as you need it, then throw it away."

Betty took a sip of coffee. "I'm not forgiving anybody."

"Don't I make the best coffee, Mother? I'll bet you've never had coffee this good at any restaurant."

"Yes, I think I needed something to eat. I'm starting to feel better already. But I'm not forgiving anybody."

"It's okay to be bitter, Mother. Keep it as long as you need it, then throw it away."

THE DECISION

"I don't know what to do now that your father's dead. Should I sell the house? Should I keep the condo in Palm Desert? If the desert weren't so warm in summer, I would live in the condo and sell this place, but you can't beat Mar Vista for climate. I love those afternoon sea breezes."

"Mother, you don't have to make any decisions now. Take your time. Let things sort themselves out."

Jake and his mother, Barbara, were sitting in the music room in his mother's house. The afternoon sun shone through the large sliding glass door that his father had installed years ago. His Hammond organ and Leslie speaker faced them as they sat side by side in two wing chairs that were covered in a bright floral pattern. A small table was between them. On it were small squares of matrimony cake, a date and oatmeal confection that his mother loved to make, together with bone china teacups filled with black tea and milk.

"I don't know why I had four children," Barbara said. "I guess I thought I was making some sort of investment in my future, but I hardly ever see them. Sharon's in Seattle, so I can't blame her for not coming all the way to L.A. to visit. Beatrice is in Dallas, so she's a long way off too. If she comes, she always brings her husband who gives himself endless airs. I suppose in our classless society, a physician still trumps a carpenter, but I hate to be reminded that they are Mr. and Mrs. Doctor and I am the very lowly and extremely humble Mrs. Carpenter."

Barbara took a sip from her teacup. "Of course, Tom is another story. I don't even want to know what his trailer in McKinleyville looks like."

"After the funeral, I drove back with Tom to McKinleyville, and you're right, there's a reason he doesn't invite you up. Bertha has a drinking problem, and their kids run wild. You wouldn't like it."

"I try to love my children, but when one lives in a run-down trailer and another is too big for her Dallas cowboy boots—Well, I try not to be judgmental. I love Tom and Beatrice. If one's a slob and the other's a snob, I don't really care. I'm glad you get along with Tom. Maybe I'll drive up to McKinleyville and surprise them. I'll give Bertha a big hug even if she's fallen down drunk."

"Why don't you let me drive you up over Thanksgiving? You can let them know you don't care how they live. We'll take them out to dinner."

"But none of this solves my problem, Jake. Should I sell the house, or should I sell the condo? I would like to keep them both, but I don't want the taxes and upkeep on two homes. Your father's pension stopped when he died, and my Social Security will stop when I start collecting your father's."

Jake hesitated a moment before speaking. "I don't like to suggest this because of what the others might think, but if you were to add my name to the deed, I would be happy to pay the taxes and upkeep on the condo. It would still be yours, and you could use it as often as you want."

"I think I will call a family conference. That's the only fair thing to do," Barbara said.

A week later, the family met at their mother's house. At their mother's insistence, Beatrice left her doctor-husband at their hotel. Tom left Bertha and their children in their trailer in McKinleyville. Sharon came from Seattle because Barbara paid her airfare. Sharon was perpetually short of money.

After dinner, the family adjourned to the living room. Jake and Tom sat beside their mother on the gold French provincial couch, and Sharon and Beatrice sat on the delicate powder-blue chairs opposite them, an arrangement which pleased their mother since she felt Jake and Tom were too large and awkward for such delicate chairs.

"As you know," Barbara began, "without your father here, I can no longer afford to keep two homes. Jake has offered to pay the taxes and upkeep on the desert condo if I add his name to the deed. It will still be my home, and I can live there whenever I wish. Jake says he has no desire to live in the desert. He doesn't even want a key."

Tom spoke up immediately, "That doesn't sound like a good idea to me. Dad always said he would love to give me the condo."

Tom was tall and thin. He was a house painter and wore old, threadbare clothes covered with paint stains. He was balding and covered his head with a baseball cap he wore backward.

"I have five kids and a wife," Tom continued. "I can barely eke out a living in McKinleyville. I know I would do better in Palm Desert. I would pay the taxes and upkeep on the condo and Mother could stay there as often as she wished. I wouldn't even ask that my name be added to the deed."

"Mother would never like that," Jake said. "Bertha's drunk half the time, and your kids never stop screaming."

"That's a lie," Tom said. "You visited us on a bad day. Bertha hardly touches a drop, and my kids are models of good behavior. I always see to that. Besides, my kids are the only grandchildren Mother has. This would give her a chance to know them better."

Barbara looked at her eldest daughter. "What do you think, Sharon?"

Sharon was a petite but slightly overweight woman in her late thirties. She wore a pink sweater, black pants, and black shoes with a low heel. She had a natural grace and elegance that contrasted her favorably with her sister.

"I would love the condo," Sharon said. "I'm tired of all the rain in Seattle. There's no reason I couldn't find a good job in the Palm Desert area. Mother could visit me as often as she wanted."

Beatrice spoke up. "I want the condo!"

Barbara was shocked. "Why would you want the condo, Beatrice? You have all the money in the world and a beautiful mansion. A three-bedroom condo would mean nothing to you."

Beatrice was never known to smile or be pleasant to anyone. Her hair was dyed platinum and short cropped. She always wore jewelry. Today, she had on a thick gold necklace and gold earrings. There was a garnet ring on her right hand, and a wedding band and a large diamond on her left.

"I will outbid everyone," Beatrice said. "I will give Mother $300,000, pay the taxes and upkeep, and let Mother stay as often as she wants. Like Jake's offer, my name will be added to Mother's on the deed."

"That makes no sense," Barbara said. "You have a condo in Manhattan and a townhouse in San Francisco. Why would you want another home in Palm Desert?"

"Of all of you, I am the only one who has been successful. Am I to be punished for my success? I'm giving Mother the best deal, so the condo is mine."

"That is the best deal," Jake said. "I withdraw my offer in favor of Beatrice's. The $300,000 will make Mother's retirement so much better. She will be able to travel and do whatever else she likes. Money makes a difference."

"That's totally unfair to me," Tom said. "I have a wife and five kids. We need a decent place to live."

"This is not about you," Jake said. "It's about Mother."

"So my kids are to starve while Mrs. Rich Witch runs off with the store!"

"You can send some of your children to live with me until you get on your feet," Barbara said.

"So I am to be completely forgotten," Sharon said. "Beatrice is intolerable. She has everything, and she wants more."

Sharon and Tom left that evening. Before Jake left the next morning, Beatrice said to him, "The rich rule the world. It's too bad the rest of you are losers."

"Don't gloat," Jake said. "It's unbecoming. However, thanks for what you did for Mother. It will make her retirement so much easier."

THE VACCINATION

Beth entered the den where her mother was seated before a table putting a hem in a dress by hand. "Mommy, can I have one of your needles, a large one?"

"Why do you need a needle?"

"I want to vacnate Jill?"

"Vacnate? What is vacnate?"

"Our teacher said everyone should be vacnated."

"You mean vaccinated," her mother corrected.

"Yes, vacnate. That's what I said."

"You vaccinate people but not dolls, Beth."

"Ms. Grundig said if you don't get vacnated, you'll get the flu. I don't want Jill to get the flu."

"Jill will not get the flu."

"Why did Ms. Grundig say that then?"

"She wants to encourage people to be vaccinated, but not dolls."

"Give me a needle, and I will vacnate Jill anyway. I don't want to take any chances."

"Jill does not need to be vaccinated."

"Ms. Grundig says if you are to be vacnated, you should be very relaxed and turn your head away from the needle, and it won't hurt. I will explain that to Jill. I don't want her to scream."

"First of all," said Beth's mother firmly, "you should not vaccinate anyone unless you are a nurse or a doctor. Now run along, Beth. Sewing is very stressful to me. We will discuss vaccination later if you still want to."

An hour later, Beth came back into the den. She was dressed in the nurse's costume she had worn on Halloween. Her mother was seated on a brown leather easy chair reading a magazine.

"Can I vacnate Jill now, Mommy? You said a nurse can vacnate."

"You have to go to school to be a nurse, Beth."

"I do go to school. I go to Dayton Heights School."

"That doesn't count. You have to go to a nursing school before you can vaccinate people."

The family's gray tabby cat was sitting on top of their old-fashioned television. His tail was hanging over the screen.

"Binky doesn't look well, Mommy. I heard him sneeze yesterday. Can we get him vacnated so he doesn't get the flu?"

"Binky is old, Beth. He had all his shots a long time ago."

"I didn't know Binky had been shot. No wonder he looks sick."

"I have to get dinner, Beth. We will talk about vaccination later."

"Ms. Grundig says vacnation is the most important thing you can do for your health. When will I get vacnated?"

"If you want to be vaccinated, I will take you to the doctor next week."

"I will do what Ms. Grundig says. I will relax completely, and I won't look at the needle. I don't want to scream."

"We're having roast beef tonight, so I need to get started right away. It needs to be done by the time your father gets home. Why don't you take off your nursing outfit and go next door and play with Lydia?"

Fifteen minutes later, Beth came into the kitchen. She was still dressed in her nursing costume. "Look, Mommy. I vacnated Jill, and I put a bandage over her arm to cover the hole."

Beth's mother seemed angry. "I'm going to have a talk with your teacher. She's scaring little children with all this talk of vaccination."

"It's not Ms. Grundig's fault, Mommy. She doesn't want us to get sick. Next week, she's going to help us look for fire hazes."

"You must mean fire hazards," Beth's mother corrected.

"That's what I said, fire hazes. Ms. Grundig says a lot of us are living in firetraps. Do you think our house is a firetrap? I don't want our house to burn down."

Beth's mother gritted her teeth. "Ms. Grundig and I are going to have a long chat very soon. I don't like her scaring little girls."

THE ECLIPSE

Louise Hallmer was sitting in her living room on a yellow sofa with a bright floral pattern. She suddenly stopped working her tablet and looked up at her husband who was sitting opposite her on a matching easy chair. "You know, Harold, I've been completely eclipsed by our daughter. She got a law degree and has a terrific job with the federal government."

"No one could eclipse you, Louise. You're too much of a dynamo."

"Don't try to pacify me, Harold. Do you know what kind of salary Alice draws?"

"But it's all due to you, Louise. Without your salary, we couldn't have afforded to pay her tuition. Alice couldn't get any scholarships and wasn't accepted by U.C.L.A. The amount of tuition you had to pay was outrageous."

"I wanted Alice to have the best education we could possibly afford. We could have bought a house with the money, but here we are, middle-aged and still just renters."

"Are you sorry?"

"No, I'm not sorry, but I am angry with myself. I should have gone to college. But my parents were against it."

"They had six kids and were dirt poor, so you really can't blame them."

"My mistake, Harold, was letting my mother bully me. Since I was the eldest, she wanted me to get a job and help with expenses. She took most of my paycheck and gave me a small allowance every week."

"I think your father was really to blame," Harold said. "He couldn't seem to hold a job."

"He was sick a lot," Louise replied, "so it wasn't really his fault. I should have left home and let my mother figure it out. She could have gotten a job. After all, she's the one that wanted six children."

"It's too bad Alice lives in D.C. We never see her."

"She telephones me almost every day. I live through her. Her success is my success. She gives me all the details about everything she does. Did you know she supervises a hundred people?"

"I think she's become the woman you wanted to be."

"How I wish I could have had a great career like Alice. I don't mind being a cashier at a supermarket, but I feel like I've wasted my life when I have so much ability."

"You didn't waste your life, Louise. Don't look at it that way. You deal with the public. You're good with people. People like you. That's a reward in itself."

"Speaking of work, I've been assigned to the early shift tomorrow, so I have to go to bed now, even though I'm not tired."

Harold sat in his easy chair alone for about half an hour, then his cell phone rang.

"Hello."

"Dad, it's Alice. I'm over at Sophie's house. Do you think you could drive over and see me?"

"What are you doing in town?"

"I'll explain later."

"You want me to drive to Glendale at this hour?"

"Yes, and don't tell Mother."

"Why not?"

"I'll explain later."

Although Louise was a sound sleeper, she might wake up and wonder where Harold was, so he taped a note to the landline telling her he had gone to the supermarket.

When Harold reached Sophie's apartment, Alice answered the door. "Oh Dad, I'm so glad to see you. I've been just miserable. Come into the kitchen so we can talk. Sophie's out for the evening, so we have complete privacy."

Harold followed Alice into the kitchen and sat down at the white wooden kitchen table.

Alice poured him some tea from a teapot and sat down. "Oh, Dad, I've done something that I know will kill Mother, but I don't know what to do about it."

"Surely nothing could be that bad."

"It's the worst thing I could have done. I've quit my wonderful, fantastic, high-paying job with the federal government."

Harold's tone of voice expressed his shock. "You didn't!"

"I did," Alice replied sadly. "I simply couldn't take the stress anymore. I was working sixteen-hour days, and yet everyone was conspiring against me. No matter how hard I worked, I seemed to be making enemies. I had no friends at management level. My staff loved me and thought I was doing a terrific job, but that didn't seem to matter with the people who counted. Many people felt my job should have been given to them, and I was made to feel their resentment."

"Your mother will be disappointed," Harold replied, "but it's your life and not hers. In a way, it will be good for her to know this. It will help her to understand that dream jobs can sometimes be nightmares. She is so resentful that she never had a college education and never landed an important job that it has made her bitter. Your failure, in the long run, might give her peace of mind, not about you but about herself."

"Oh, Dad, I feel more awful than you can ever imagine. I know how badly Mother wanted me to succeed and how much my tuition cost. I owe everything to her, and yet I've let her down."

"The important thing, Alice, is that you must not let yourself down. If you weren't happy, then you did the right thing by leaving. There will be other jobs, and some of them will work out for you."

"But there is one other thing, Dad."

"What's that?"

"I'm pregnant."

Harold's voice showed his surprise. "Pregnant!"

"Yes, pregnant. A man at work was in the same unhappy position I was. We would both get together and moan about how unhappy we were. There were a few nights when we had too much bourbon. Considering all the stress I was under, I just wanted to forget how unhappy I was. I really don't want to tell mother about my failure at my job, and I certainly don't want to tell her that I'm pregnant."

"Are you going to have the baby?"

"I want the baby more than anything. Stan is married, but he's given me some money. I'm going to Spain. When I return, I will tell everyone about the child I will claim I adopted. No one needs to know the truth, least of all Mother."

"What shall I tell your mother then?"

"You don't have to say anything. I'll drop in tomorrow and tell Mother I'm taking a sabbatical and going to Europe."

Harold had to work the next day, but when he came home, Louise was waiting for him at the front door to tell him the news.

"Harold, come in and sit down."

Harold entered the house and sat down on the yellow floral sofa.

"The most amazing thing has happened," Louise continued, "Alice stopped by. She had very little time. It turns out her work for the government has been so extraordinary that she has been awarded a sabbatical. She is going to Europe to paint. You know how much she loves to draw."

"Do you think Alice might be a government spy?" Harold asked in jest.

Louise seemed flustered for a moment, then she said, "Oh, Harold, you and your silly jokes. Of course Alice is not a spy."

Louise paused before continuing, "Oh how I wish all this could have happened to me. If my parents had let me go to college, I could have had the wonderful life Alice has. No stress, no worries. Just money and happiness from a rewarding career."

"I'm sure Alice has her problems," Harold said.

"How could Alice have any problems? People at that level never have problems. As I said, Alice has no stress, no worries. Just money and happiness from a rewarding career. I couldn't be happier for her, even if she has completely eclipsed me."

BIRTHDAYS

Ellen Jensen was sitting on a blue damask wing chair in the study when she suddenly put her crossword puzzle on a small table next to her chair. "Burt, I hate birthdays!"

Burt Jensen turned away from his computer. "Me too. I wish they would go away."

"That's not what I mean," Ellen replied. "I hate birthdays because I hate buying presents for people. I bought that pink blouse for your mother, and I doubt if she liked it. I've never seen her wear it. She probably regifted it."

"Amelia was wearing it when I was over at her house. She said Mother didn't like the puffy sleeves."

"See what I mean. You can't please people. I paid $59.95 for that blouse. What a waste of money."

"Next time, buy Mother something from the 99-Cent Store. It will teach her a lesson."

"The 99-Cent Store! That's not a very good joke. Your mother won't even look at a gift if she thinks you bought it on the cheap."

"Mother's what I call a 'money snob,'" Burt replied. "She values things by what they cost. She probably thought you bought the blouse at a discount store. Next time, leave the price tag on."

"That seems so vulgar, but I know what you mean. Your mother is always telling me the price she paid for things. Did you know she paid $5,000 for that armoire in her bedroom?"

"Yes, and it's hand carved and comes from Italy."

"She claims her couch cost three thousand dollars," Ellen said, "but I don't believe it."

"It couldn't have cost three thousand. I think Mother does a little fibbing from time to time."

"Now I have to decide what to get Billy for his birthday. He says he wants a car."

"He can use one of ours."

"We use ours to go to work, so Billy has to take the bus to school," Ellen replied. "He says the kids laugh at him because of it."

"I knew we shouldn't have bought a house in this neighborhood," Burt said. "The people here are all money snobs just like Mother."

"You wanted to impress your mother."

"I did, but every time I make a mortgage payment, I hate myself."

"If Billy feels humiliated because he has to take the bus to school, I suppose we'll have to buy him a car. Perhaps I can find a nice used one. I'll look around."

"I hate taking on any more debt."

Ellen saw Billy standing in the doorway. "We were just talking about your birthday, Billy. We've decided to get you a car after all."

Billy smiled. "I already have a car, Mom."

"You already have a car? What do you mean?"

"I told Granny how hard up you were, and she's decided to give me her Mercedes. She wants a new car anyway."

"Now I feel humiliated," Burt said. "Mother will jump on me and say I'm a failure."

"Well, I did have to lay it on a little thick, Dad. I said you and Mom were bankrupt and had been getting your food from food banks."

Burt looked angry. "How could you say something like that Billy?"

"Don't worry about your Mother," Ellen said. "Let's just be glad Billy has a car. Now the next question, Billy, is what do you want for your birthday? Something not too expensive, I hope, since you've already told your grandma we're bankrupt."

"Well, since I've already saved you two a fortune by coming up with a car on my own, I've already told all my friends you're giving me a round-the-world tour when I graduate. I want to see everything: the Great Wall of China, the Taj Mahal, the Kremlin, the Egyptian pyramids, everything."

Burt groaned, but Ellen smiled.

"We have over a year to save up for it," Ellen said, "and we can always max out our credit cards. After all, we only have one son."

"I'm glad we never went to the fertility clinic," Burt replied. "One son is about all I can handle."

THE ATM MACHINE

Lyle was sitting in the yellow floral-patterned easy chair in the living room when his daughter entered the house. "It's about time you came home, Pamela! We've been waiting up all night for you!"

"Don't be upset, Father. It's only two in the morning."

"Only two in the morning! You know we expect you to be in by midnight."

"This is the twenty-first century, Father. Girls can't be ordered around like they were a hundred years ago. We've earned the right to vote and the right to stay out as long as we want."

Gwen was seated on the yellow floral-patterned sofa near Lyle. "Don't start an argument, Pamela. Your father's concerned for your welfare. He's not trying to run your life."

"Why are you taking his side, Mother? Don't agree with him just because he's a man."

"I'm not agreeing with him. I think you should be home by midnight."

"Rules! Rules! Rules! All I get are rules."

"Stop this nonsense," Gwen replied. "Just be home by midnight the next time."

"Well, I won't have to obey Dad's silly rules much longer. Allen Wexford proposed to me tonight."

"Then you'll have to obey his silly rules," Lyle said, "and they'll be a great deal tougher than mine."

"Nonsense. I'm not obeying anyone's rules. Allen adores me because I'm independent. He likes a woman who takes charge."

"He does look like a wimp," Lyle said. "Are you sure you want a man you can walk all over?"

"Allen has money, and he spends it on me. That's all I care about."

"Well, if Allen has money, then I approve of the marriage," Gwen said. "Your father and I have always struggled financially. I wouldn't wish poverty on anyone."

"We're not poor," Lyle said. "This is a nice house, and we own it free and clear."

"Well, we don't live under a freeway bridge if that's what you mean," Gwen replied. "but we don't live in Bel Air either."

"Not everyone can be filthy rich," Lyle said.

Gwen smiled. "If Pamela is to become filthy rich, then I'm happy for her."

"That's good," Pamela said, "because I expect you two to fork over some dough for the big wedding I plan to have."

"Fork over some dough!" Lyle exclaimed. "It isn't as though we can just cook up some money in the kitchen."

"I didn't want Allen to think you were poor," Pamela replied, "so I told him you had inherited ten million from your father but preferred to live humbly in this simple, old-fashioned house."

"Are you sure Allen's not marrying you for our alleged millions?" Gwen asked.

"Well, I had to snag him somehow," Pamela said.

Lyle frowned. "I don't think a marriage should be based on a lie. I'll tell Allen the true state of our finances, and you can see if he's still interested."

"Don't you dare! I've worked hard to get this proposal. I'm not letting you two ruin it."

"We'll pay for a modest wedding and nothing more," Lyle said.

"I'm having a big wedding at the Four Seasons Hotel in Beverly Hills. There will be seven bridesmaids and two hundred guests."

Lyle's face flushed red. "I'm not funding this."

"Don't be hasty," Gwen said. "We have a lot of retirement money in our 401(k)s. We could use some of that."

"What about our retirement?"

"Oh, we'll probably be dead by then. Let's not begrudge Pamela a nice wedding. I never had one, and I regret it."

"Your parents were dirt poor. How could they afford a big wedding?"

"Well, your parents could have chipped in. They weren't poor. Our wedding was such a miserable, little hole-in-the-wall affair. I want Pamela to have a wedding she can be proud of."

The next evening, Pamela came home by midnight. Lyle and Gwen were seated in the living room waiting for her.

"Thank you for coming home on time," Lyle said.

"I didn't do it because of you. I did it because of Allen. He told me he was an airline pilot, but it turns out he's just a baggage handler."

"Do you still want a big wedding?"

"Of course, but not with Allen. So save up some dough."

Lyle smiled. "I guess you'll have to look around for another ATM machine."

"That's not a nice thing to say. It makes me sound like a gold digger. I don't mind going out with Allen, but I've decided not to get serious."

Gwen spoke, "Don't be hard on Pamela, Lyle. She needs to marry a man with a future. Life is hard if you don't have any money."

"That's what I said," Lyle replied. "Pamela needs to look around for another ATM machine."

"Father, you are positively evil. I haven't dumped Allen. I'm just not getting serious."

"Maybe you should marry a bank," Lyle said, "or better yet, a whole chain of banks."

Pamela looked at her mother. "How do you put up with him?"

"I don't know," Gwen replied. "I just always have."

Painting in Oils

Jason opened the door to Clarissa's studio which he had been warned never to enter, but he did so anyway.

Clarissa was standing before one of her paintings, which was on an easel. "Jason, what are you doing here? You know I don't want you in my studio."

"My curiosity got the better of me, Clarissa. You spend so much of your time in here it makes me feel like I'm single."

"Perhaps you are single," Clarissa said sharply. "If I'm married to anyone, it's to my art." Clarissa's voice softened. "Well, since you're here, you might as well take a look at my latest painting. You won't have the intelligence or refinement to understand it, but I'll let you see it anyway."

Jason studied the canvas. He knew anything he said would reflect on him negatively, but he felt he had to say something, so he said, "I think the painting is interesting."

"Interesting! Is that all you can say? Would you call a Picasso interesting or a Pollock?"

"Well, it has many fine points, Clarissa, but I'm not really an expert on art."

"Don't you love the colors? That shade of green is perfect. It sends shivers down my spine."

"Yes, I like the green, but I'm not sure what the painting's about."

"Not sure what the painting's about! How can you say that! It's a portrait of our daughter, Debbie."

Jason studied the painting carefully. He felt he had to lie a little. "Yes, I see that now, but why does she have three arms?"

"That's symbolism. Debbie's arms are stretched out in love. Because she loves me so much, I felt she needed three arm to express it. Perhaps I should have given her four or five arms, but I have a tendency to be conservative."

"There's a silver ball above Debbie with wings. What is that about?"

"I think that should be obvious, but since you don't know anything about art, I'll explain it. The silver ball with wings, as you call it, is Debbie's fairy godmother. Debbie saw a story on television with a fairy godmother in it, and she's been talking about her fairy godmother ever since. Because it's so much a part of Debbie, I felt I had to include it."

"How come there's a hand that comes out of Debbie's forehead?"

"Oh, Jason, I am so disappointed in you. That is one of the most obvious symbols in the painting. The hand coming out of Debbie's forehead refers to Debbie's kindness and her desire to help others. For a five-year-old, she is remarkable."

Jason felt he had to continue to lie to please Clarissa. "Yes, it's all quite good. I see it clearly now. You're nothing less than a genius when you paint."

"I'm glad you're so perceptive, Jason. The art critic Creswell Crisp would agree with your assessment. He told me just last week that I have a great deal of talent. He didn't use the word genius, but I think that's what he meant."

"I've made some macaroni and cheese. Would you like some?"

"Thank goodness I have a husband who cooks," Clarissa replied. "I'll join you in the kitchen after I clean up."

Jason decided not to go into Clarissa's studio again. He didn't understand what she was doing, but after all, he knew nothing about art. At best, he might say something stupid. At worst, he might say something that would subject him to merciless ridicule.

A week later, Clarissa said, "I've taken some money out of our savings account."

"Why?" Jason asked.

"Cresswell Crisp wants to exhibit some of my paintings at a show he's doing."

"Why can't he just exhibit them? Why does he need the money?"

"He's having a cash flow problem at his gallery. The rent is due, so he needs a little extra cash right now."

"I don't think you should give him any money."

"Why not? Creswell is convinced my paintings will sell. He has a well-heeled clientele. He's putting a price of fifty thousand on my portrait of Debbie."

"Do people really pay that much for art?"

"Of course, you ignoramus. Once the buzz gets out about my work, I'll not only be famous, I'll be wealthy."

Three months later, when they were sitting in the kitchen, Jason said, "I need some money to pay our property taxes. Did you ever put any money back into the bank?"

"Creswell told me last week that he sold my portrait of Debbie and promised to send me a check. I telephoned him yesterday, but there was no answer."

"Let's drive over to the gallery then and talk to him."

"Yes, let's do. The check's probably in the mail, but perhaps he's sold another of my paintings, and I can collect on that. I'll take Debbie next door, and Brenda can watch her while we're gone."

When Jason and Clarissa arrived at Creswell's gallery, it was closed.

"The gallery seems to be empty," Clarissa said as she peered through the front window.

"Wait here, Clarissa. I'll go around to the back alley and see if a door or window is open, then I'll let you in."

Jason walked to the end of the block. Then he went down the alley to the rear of Creswell Crisp's store. The door and windows were locked, but there was a large dumpster pressed against the back wall of the gallery. He opened the dumpster and saw a number of paintings in cheap wooden frames. He fished through them and found the portrait of Debbie. It was badly damaged. He decided not to tell Clarissa.

When Jason rejoined Clarissa at the front of the gallery, she said, "I see it all clearly now. Cresswell sold all my paintings at massive prices and no longer has to work. He probably purchased a villa in Italy with the proceeds from my paintings."

"He probably did," Jason replied.

"That's the trouble with being a genius," Clarissa said. "Everyone takes advantage of you."

"It seems that way," Jason replied.

"Van Gogh never made any money in his lifetime, and it will probably be the same with me, but when I die, my paintings will be worth millions."

"I'm sure they will," Jason replied. "I'm sure they will."

THE CATERPILLAR

Jason found his father in the garage making a wooden chair for a neighbor. "Dad, I need to talk to you."

Lester turned away from his work. "What is it, Jason?"

"My teacher at school said a caterpillar turns into a butterfly. I don't see how that's possible."

"Is that what they teach you in the seventh grade?"

"The teacher just mentioned it in English class. I wondered if she was just kidding or if it's something that really happens."

"It really happens, but I'm not a science guy," Lester replied. "Why don't you ask your mother if you want to know more about it? She thinks she knows everything."

Jason found his mother in the kitchen. "Mother, can you tell me how a caterpillar turns into a butterfly?"

Harriette turned from the kitchen sink and looked toward Jason. "I paid a great deal of money for that iPad I bought you for Christmas. Don't you ever use it?"

"I thought it would be easier if you explained it to me."

"Look it up on your iPad, but let me just say this: this house is a caterpillar, but if your father would get off his duff and paint it, it would be a butterfly."

"You think the house is a caterpillar?"

"The outside of the house is starting to peel, but instead of painting it, your father is making a dining-room suite for that horrible Beverly Sims down the street."

"What's wrong with Mrs. Sims?"

"She knows your father is a carpenter, and she wants new dining-room furniture. If I know Beverly, she'll hardly pay him a penny."

Jason's sister was two years older than Jason. When she came home from school, Jason told her how their house was a caterpillar, but it could be a butterfly if it were painted.

"Poor Dad," Lorena said. "He's so busy making furniture for the neighbors he doesn't have time to paint a house."

"I hate to see Mother living in a caterpillar," Jason said.

There was a pause, then Lorena said, "Why don't we paint the house ourselves? Mother's going to visit Aunt Sadie in Palm Desert next week, and Dad will be away at work."

"What about the places where the paint is peeling?"

"You can use Dad's sander to fix that."

"We don't have any paint or brushes."

"I'll buy some at the hardware store. Since I'm afraid of heights, you can paint the high parts of the house, and I'll paint the low places."

A week later, Jason and Lorena began working on the house. Jason did the sanding first, then he climbed up the ladder to paint under the eaves.

Painting wasn't easy. It got in Jason's hair and on his clothes. The house seemed to soak up the paint. It splashed everywhere.

The house was only one story, so there was no great danger from heights. But when Jason tried to stand on the front porch roof to paint the gable, he slipped on the sloped porch roof and landed on the driveway. Lorena telephoned her father who took Jason to the Emergency Room.

When Harriette came home from Palm Desert, she found a partly-painted house and a son working his iPad in the den with a cast on his leg.

"I'm furious with your father for this," Harriette said. "He should have painted the house himself instead of making furniture for that horrible Beverly Sims."

"Why is making furniture wrong?"

"Your father will stand on his head for any pretty woman he sees, but he won't do a thing for me."

"I've googled caterpillars and butterflies on my iPad. Do you want to know about it?"

"Not today. I'm tired from rushing home from Palm Desert. Your father should have telephoned me on the day of the accident, but he didn't even have that courtesy. You can tell me all about caterpillars and butterflies another time."

LEAVING TOWN

Howard and Ellen Springwood were watching television in their living room when Howard suddenly put the television on hold using the remote.

"Ellen, did you hear about the Barkers next door?"

"No, what about them?"

"They're going to Europe next week."

"What, again?"

"Boyd tells me this will be their tenth trip. They plan to stay a full month. They're doing Vienna, Florence, and Venice."

"Why don't we ever go to Europe?"

"With only one salary, how can we afford it? Melissa has a terrific job."

"So I'm at fault, is that it? If you had a better job, we could take a vacation once in awhile. We haven't even been to Vegas."

"We went to Palm Springs last year."

"That was only because the Hennegans put us up."

"Two salaries make a difference, Ellen. The Barkers just bought a place in Beverly Hills. It's being renovated while they're away. They plan to move in as soon as they return."

"Why do you tell me these things, Howard? Are you trying to make me miserable? We live in a crummy neighborhood while the Barkers move to a palace in Beverly Hills."

"We did raise a successful son."

"Yes, but he doesn't give us a penny. A lot of good that did us."

"Bert's a good boy," Howard said.

"Of course he is, and I love him, but I gave up my career as a dancer just to be a mom."

"You couldn't dance now with your arthritis."

"Howard, why don't you shut up? Everything you say makes me miserable."

Howard switched the television on using the remote, and he and Ellen continued watching their program.

Two weeks later when Howard returned home from work, Ellen met him at the door.

"The Barkers must have come home early from Europe, Howard."

"Why do you say that?"

"A moving van pulled up and took their furniture away. They have a lot of beautiful things, including a magnificent grandfather clock. I stood on the sidewalk as they loaded up the van. They have a beautiful Victorian living-room suite covered in red velvet and a large canopy bed that must have cost a fortune. I went inside the Barkers' house and watched the movers dismantle it. They didn't seem to mind me being nosey. Melissa has a china cabinet crammed full of exquisite porcelain. I would have loved to look at each piece to see the identifying marks underneath, but I didn't dare."

"Our furniture's not so bad."

"Yes, we have nice furniture, but nothing like Melissa's. I love my Russian tea service and my Francis I sterling silver, but I would gladly trade everything I have for what the Barkers have."

"If I know you, Ellen, you would want your things and Melissa's."

Ellen smiled. "Am I that transparent?"

Two weeks later, the doorbell rang. Ellen answered the door. It was Melissa Barker.

"Melissa, how wonderful to see you. You must come in and tell us about your trip to Europe. We're having coffee and dessert in the dining room. You're welcome to join us if you wish."

Melissa seemed agitated. "No, I can't stay. I just have to ask you a few questions."

Melissa sat down on the blue damask couch, which Ellen noted was not nearly as nice as the red velvet Victorian. Howard and Ellen sat opposite Melissa in matching easy chairs.

Melissa spoke: "Did either of you notice a moving van come to my house a few weeks ago?"

"Of course I did," Ellen replied. "The moving men were quite wonderful. They let me watch the whole process. I never knew you had so much beautiful porcelain."

"Well, there's a big problem," Melissa said. "While we were in Europe, someone called a moving company and took all our furniture, everything. We don't know who it was. We don't even know the name of the moving company. You don't happen to remember the name of the company, do you?"

"No, my mind's a blank on that," Ellen replied. "I was so enthralled by all your beautiful things that I didn't notice the name on the truck."

"What about your move to Beverly Hills?" Howard asked.

"That's another problem," Melissa replied. "Boyd thought there was more money in our checking account than there actually was because I had written a large check and forgot to put it in the register, so the check he wrote for the down payment bounced. It seems our escrow is in some sort of limbo."

"What will you do?" Ellen asked.

"We can't do anything because we don't have enough for the down payment," Melissa replied. "There was a million dollars hidden in the furniture because Boyd doesn't trust banks. They snoop for the government you know, and the government taxes us to death. I'm sure you understand what I'm saying."

"Have you called the police?" Howard asked.

"We don't want to get the police involved in this."

"Melissa, I'm so sorry," Ellen said. "Is there any way we can help?"

"No, we're okay, I guess. Boyd's out now buying sleeping bags. At least we still have a house."

A month later, Howard and Ellen were watching the eight o'clock news. A couple, identified as Boyd and Melissa Barker, were found shot to death in their car by an unknown assailant. Ellen started to cry.

"Don't be upset, Ellen. We don't have a million dollars hidden in our furniture, so we should be okay. We may not be as wealthy as the Barkers were, but we've always been honest."

Ellen smiled through her tears. "I would have loved to have that beautiful living-room suite and that large canopy bed, but I suppose it's not worth dying for."

"Let's go into debt and go to Vegas," Howard said.

"Yes, let's," Ellen replied. "We deserve a vacation. Life's too short not to have some fun."

WATCHING TELEVISION

Damon was sitting on the yellow floral-patterned couch watching TV when his mother, Henrietta, stormed into the living room and turned the television off. "Damon, I've warned you, you're watching too much television."

"Mother, I like to watch television. I learn a lot about acting."

"Some of these shows are simply pornography and full of foul language. The lawn needs mowing, the cars need to be washed, and you probably haven't even touched your homework. You're nineteen and still in high school. This is ridiculous. When I grew up, we did our chores with a smile, and we always did our homework."

"Mother, you were a saint and a straight A student. How could I ever be compared with you?"

Henrietta smiled. "I was extremely bright, and if my parents hadn't brainwashed me into having children, I probably would have had a fantastic career."

"You only had one child."

"A wise woman once said, 'Zero children is not enough, and one child is too many.' I learned that lesson before I had a second child."

"Don't you like being a mother?"

"Of course I like being a mother, but when you have a son who sits around all day and watches television while you cook and clean like a madwoman, you begin to wonder if it's all worth it."

The front door opened, and Damon's father, Richard, entered the living room. "Damon, how come the lawn hasn't been mowed and the trees trimmed?"

"I will get to it tomorrow."

"Tomorrow's not good enough. If I were smart, I'd stop your allowance."

"It's only a dollar, Dad. That's no big deal."

"Don't answer back, Damon. I expect you to treat your father with respect."

"Mother tells me she's sorry she had me. How do you think that makes me feel?"

Henrietta raised her voice. "I did not tell Damon I was sorry I had him. I simply said one LAZY, LAZY, LAZY boy was all I could handle."

"I'm in the twelfth grade," Damon said, "and you haven't even bought me a car."

"You don't deserve a car," Richard replied. "Until you improve your grades and do the yard work, I won't even consider getting you a car."

"I try real hard at school, but a lot of it just doesn't interest me."

"A 'D' average just doesn't cut it."

"I think you two would like me better if I committed suicide."

Henrietta's voice was full of compassion. "No, no, no, Damon. Don't do that. It would destroy me."

Richard said, "I'm not easily fooled. You're just bluffing."

"I'm not bluffing," Damon replied. "Susan can get me poison from her chemistry class."

"I don't know why you hang around that girl," Henrietta said.

"She has a nice body," Damon replied.

"Is that what all this television teaches you? You should admire a girl for her mind but not her body," Henrietta said.

"I can't see a mind," Damon replied.

"I'm being emotionally blackmailed," Henrietta said. "I don't want to be blamed for a suicide, so just keep watching television all you want. I simply don't care anymore."

"Henrietta, Damon has to do something around here," Richard said.

"No, he doesn't. If he wants to ruin his life, that's up to him."

Henrietta had turned the television off; but now, with a big smile, Damon turned it on again with the remote. Henrietta and Richard left the room.

The next week, Damon announced he was moving in with a theatrical agent in Hollywood. He wouldn't give his parents any details and wouldn't leave an address or phone number. He returned his cell phone to his parents and didn't contact them again.

"I guess I've failed," Henrietta said. "I wanted the best for Damon, but this is how it ends up."

"I don't trust those Hollywood types," Richard said. "It's all drinking and drugs and loose living."

A year later, when Henrietta and Richard were watching television, they were amazed when they saw Damon on the television screen in a sitcom.

"I wanted my son to be a doctor or a lawyer," Richard said, "but it seems we have an actor."

"It must be his good looks that got him the part," Henrietta replied. "Of course, he got his exceptional appearance from my side of the family."

"My family's not ugly."

"Well, they're not good looking either."

"Henrietta, stop this. Let's just be happy that Damon's found his niche. It's not what we wanted, but it will have to do."

"I hope he telephones sometime so I can let him know how proud I am."

"I guess you were a successful mother after all," Richard said.

Henrietta smiled but said nothing.

CPSIA information can be obtained
at www.ICGtesting.com
Printed in the USA
FSHW010315090921
84574FS